SIMON SPOTLIGHT
An imprint of Simon & Schuster Children's Publishing Division
1230 Avenue of the Americas, New York, New York 10020

Based on the TV series *Rugrats*® created by Klasky/Csupo Inc. and
Paul Germain as seen on Nickelodeon®

First Simon Spotlight Edition, 1998

Manufactured in the United States of America

10 9 8 7 6 5 4 3 2 1

Library of Congress Cataloging-in-Publication Data
Albee, Sarah.
Space invaders! / by Sarah Albee ; illustrated by Ron Zalme. — 1st ed.
p.   cm. — (Ready-to-read)
"Based on the TV series, Rugrats, created by Klasky/Csupo Inc. and
Paul Germain as seen on Nickelodeon"—T.p. verso.
Summary: The Rugrats babies become convinced that Earth is about to be
invaded by space aliens.
ISBN 0-689-82130-1 (pbk.)
[1. Babies—Fiction. 2. Extraterrestrial beings—Fiction.]
I. Zalme, Ron, ill. II. Title. III. Series.
PZ7.A3174Sp   1998
97-44205
[Fic]—DC21
CIP   AC

Space Invaders!

By Sarah Albee

Illustrated by Ron Zalme

Ready-to-Read

Simon Spotlight/Nickelodeon

"Tommy, they're after us!" cried Chuckie. He ducked under a pillow.

"Aw, it's just the TV, Chuckie," said Tommy. "The space invaders are not really coming to get us."

"Watch out," said a space creature on TV. "YOU might be NEXT! Ha! Ha! Ha! Ha! Haaaaaaa!"

Chuckie jumped off the couch. He hid behind a curtain. "They'll be here any minute!" he said.

Suddenly, Chuckie saw something out the window. "Uh-oh . . ." he said.

"What, Chuckie?" asked Tommy.

Chuckie pointed. A big scary thing with three legs stood in the backyard.

Chuckie wailed, "We're doomed! The space invaders are here!"

"We won't let them take anyone!" Tommy said bravely.

"*We?*" asked Chuckie in a worried voice.

Just then, Chaz walked into the room. "Thanks for watching Chuckie, Didi," he called. "I hope there's space at the craft show."

Chaz gave his son a hug. "See ya later, Chuckie!" he said.

Chuckie looked at Tommy. "My dad's getting a spacecraft!" he groaned.

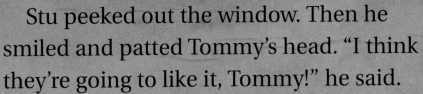

Stu peeked out the window. Then he smiled and patted Tommy's head. "I think they're going to like it, Tommy!" he said.

Stu stomped back downstairs.

"They know too, Tommy," Chuckie said. "They're going away with the space invaders!"

Didi stepped out of the bathroom.
"Are you boys playing nicely?" she asked.
"There's so much to do before they get here!"

"We hafta do something, Tommy," Chuckie said.

"Don't worry, Chuckie," said Tommy. "I'll think of something."

Suddenly, Betty barged in with Phil
and Lil. She put all the babies into the
playpen. "Nice shirt, Chuckie," she said.
"It's perfect for later!"

"Oh, no," Chuckie whimpered.

"Well, time for my marching orders!"
Betty added, before going into the kitchen.

"Martian orders! Did you hear that?" said Chuckie. "Phil, Lil, your mom is becoming a Martian!"

"Why?" asked Phil.

"'Cause the space invaders are gonna take them all away!" Chuckie cried.

The babies were so busy worrying, they didn't notice Stu carrying something out to the backyard.

A little later, Spike trotted in. He had something in his mouth.

"Look! Spike has a space helmet!" cried Tommy. "Spike must've had a fight with the space invader and taken his helmet!"

Tommy quickly opened the playpen. The babies hurried to the window. They thought they would see the space invader lying on the grass. But they saw something else.

"Another space invader!" Chuckie
squeaked.

Sure enough, some other strange thing
was in the backyard. It had blinking lights.
It had bouncy springs. Little puffs of
smoke came out of its head.

"We have no choice," said Tommy. "We have to talk to the space invaders."

"What are you going to tell them, Tommy?" asked Lil.

"I'll tell them they can't have our moms and dads," said Tommy. Then he spoke slowly through the open door. "Attention, please! We are friendly earthlings. Please don't take away our moms and dads!"

Peep-peep! went the space invader.

Woosh-woosh.

Click-click.

"It's TALKING to us!" yelled Lil.

SPLICK!
Something red squirted out from it,
right at the babies.

"It's FIRING at us!" yelled Phil.

"We're doomed, doomed, doomed!"
wailed Chuckie.

"Waaaah!" yelled the babies. Stu, Didi, and Betty rushed to see what was wrong— just as the doorbell rang.

"It's THEM!" cried Chuckie.

The babies wailed again, "WAAAAAH!"

Stu picked up Tommy. "Gee, I wonder what's bothering the kids?" he said. "Maybe they want to see what's outside. I think they're gonna be blown away!"

"WAAAAAHHH!" yelled the babies, even louder than before.

Everyone trooped outside. All the babies had their eyes closed.

"Look, Tommy," said Stu. Tommy opened one eye. He saw Stu pointing to the space invader.

"Here's the friendly ketchup, mustard, and relish machine!" Stu said proudly. "Nifty, huh?"

The babies looked at one another.

SPLICK! went the machine. Ketchup squirted all over Stu and Tommy.

"Okay, so I have to work out a few kinks," said Stu.

Tommy laughed. So did Chuckie, Phil, and Lil.

Soon everyone was in the backyard. "Great day for a barbecue, Didi," said Mr. Carmichael. "And that's uh, a very interesting invention, Stu." Mr. Carmichael looked down at the blob of ketchup on his shirt.

"Thanks!" said Stu.

"Yep. These are great hot dogs, Deed," said Betty. "And the hamburgers are out of this world!"